The King's Pudding

Retold by Mairi Mackinnon
Illustrated by Nathalie Ragondet

Reading consultant: Alison Kelly
University of Roehampton

Little Deer lived in a **dangerous** jungle.

SNAP!

One morning, he went to the river to drink.

Suddenly, something caught his eye.

"Tiger!" gasped Little Deer.

"Breakfast!" growled Tiger.

Little Deer looked
around quickly.

"Oh no, I can't possibly b
your breakfast," he said

"I'm guarding the King's pudding."

"The King's pudding?" asked Tiger.

Little Deer pointed to a brownish cake on the ground.

It's the most delicious thing you ever tasted.

"No one else is allowed to go near it."

10

"You mean I can't even
try it?" asked Tiger.

11

"Oh no," said Little Deer.
"The King would be
furious."

"You could pretend you
didn't see me," said Tiger.

"I know!" said Little Deer.
"I could pretend you
chased me away."

Brilliant!

And Little Deer ran away,
as fast as he could.

15

Tiger closed his eyes
and licked the pudding.

Bleurgh!

It was just a heap of mud.

"Little Deer, wait until I catch you!" he growled.

But Little Deer was safe, far, far away.

In the middle of the day,
Little Deer went to the
river to drink.

Suddenly, something
caught his eye.

"Tiger!" gasped Little Deer.

"Lunch!" growled Tiger.

Little Deer looked around.
"Oh no, I can't possibly be
your lunch."

"I'm guarding the King's belt."

"The King's belt?" asked Tiger.

Little Deer pointed to a
bright loop hanging over
a branch.

23

"No one else is allowed
to touch it."

"You mean I can't even
try it on?" asked Tiger.

25

"Oh no," said Little Deer.
"The King would be
furious."

"The King won't know,"
said Tiger. "I won't tell."

"But someone else might see," said Little Deer.

"Let's pretend you chased me away."

Good idea!

And Little Deer ran away,
as fast as he could.

Tiger draped the belt around his waist. He pulled it tight.

Yowww!

The belt hissed. It was a snake, a very angry snake.

"Little Deer, wait until I catch you!" growled Tiger.

But Little Deer was safe, far, far away.

That evening, Little Deer
went to the river to drink.

Suddenly, something
caught his eye.

"Tiger!" gasped
Little Deer.

"Dinner!"
growled Tiger.

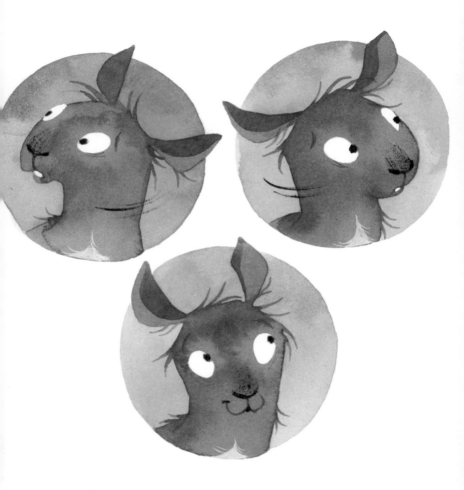

Little Deer looked around.
"Oh no, I can't possibly be
your dinner."

"I'm guarding the King's drum."

"The King's drum?" asked Tiger.

It's the finest drum in the land!

Little Deer pointed to a dark shape hanging from a tree.

"No one else is allowed
to touch it."

"You mean I can't even tap it?" asked Tiger.

"Oh no," said Little Deer. "The King would be furious."

"You could say you didn't
see me," said Tiger.

"That's no good,"
said Little Deer.

"I need to be far, far away,
so I can't even hear you."

And Little Deer ran
away, as fast as he could.

42

Tiger patted the shape.
Wasps poured out of their
nest, buzzing angrily.

They stung poor Tiger
again and again.

"Little Deer!" roared
Tiger. "I give up!"

"My mouth is full of mud."

"My tummy is full of
snake bites..."

"...and my paws are full
of wasp stings."

"I promise I will never try to eat you again!"

Far, far away, Little
Deer heard Tiger's roar
and smiled.

The King's Pudding is a story from Indonesia. Little Deer is a tiny mouse deer, between 20-30cm (about 8-12 inches) tall.

Designed by Caroline Spatz
Series designer: Russell Punter
Series editor: Lesley Sims

First published in 2012 by Usborne Publishing Ltd., Usborne House, 83-85 Saffron Hill, London EC1N 8RT, England. www.usborne.com
Copyright © 2012 Usborne Publishing Ltd.